TALES FROM
PERCY'S PARK

NICK BUTTERWORTH

Collins

An imprint of HarperCollins*Publishers*

Tales from Percy's Park contains:

THE CROSS RABBIT
THE FOX'S HICCUPS
THE BADGER'S BATH
THE HEDGEHOG'S BALLOON

First published in Great Britain by HarperCollins Publishers Ltd in 1996
2 4 6 8 10 9 7 5 3 2 1
This edition © Nick Butterworth 1996
The Cross Rabbit was first published by HarperCollins Publishers Ltd in 1995
The Fox's Hiccups was first published by HarperCollins Publishers Ltd in 1995
The Badger's Bath was first published by HarperCollins Publishers Ltd in 1996
The Hedgehog's Balloon was first published by HarperCollins Publishers Ltd in 1996
A CIP record for this title is available from the British Library
The author asserts the moral right to be identified as the author of the work
ISBN: 0 00 198208 7
Printed and bound in Italy

THE CROSS RABBIT

It was a bright, cold winter's day. Snow had fallen in the night and now everything in the park had been turned into a guessing game.

"It looks wonderful," said Percy the park keeper, "but it makes a lot of work."

Standing next to Percy was a rather old and cross looking rabbit.

"Well, quite so," said the rabbit. "But now, what about these mice? They're making a dreadful nuisance of themselves."

Percy found it hard not to laugh
when he saw what was making
the rabbit so cross.

The mice were having great fun.

Percy began to chuckle, but quickly
turned the chuckle into a cough. After
all, this was no fun for an old rabbit
who only wanted to curl up and sleep
through the cold weather.

"Now come along, you mice," said Percy. "You must go and play somewhere else. And," he added, "try to stay out of mischief."

The mice looked very disappointed. Slowly they walked away, dragging their toboggans behind them.

The old rabbit said thank you to Percy and then disappeared into his burrow.

Percy got on with clearing the snow. It was hot work even in the cold weather. First he took off his cap. Then his scarf. And then, even his gloves.

Percy worked hard all morning. He mopped his brow again and looked at his work.

"Very good," he said to himself. "I think I deserve a spot of lunch."

Percy reached for his bag and pulled out a flask.

"That's funny," he said. "I'm sure I put the cup on the top this morning."

"I know, I'll have my yogurt first and drink from the empty carton."

Percy took out a strawberry yogurt and began to rummage through his bag.

"That's odd," he said.

"No spoon. Hmm."

It was a strange lunch. A lid was missing from a small box of dates and the bottom half of one of Percy's cheese rolls had disappeared. And Percy was sure he had packed an orange but there was no sign of it now. It was all very puzzling.

It felt colder to Percy as he went back to work. He reached for his scarf and his cap, but now they had disappeared too!

" **T**his is most peculiar," said Percy. Then, as he gazed around looking for his cap and scarf, Percy was amazed to see his gloves walking off by themselves!

"I must be dreaming," said Percy.

"I'd like to be dreaming," said a cross voice. It was the old rabbit again.
"Those mice are making a terrible noise. Would you speak to them please?" And with that the rabbit stumped off.

Percy followed.

"Look!" said the rabbit.
Percy looked. The mice had been
very busy indeed! And they were having
a marvellous time.

"Hello Percy!" they called. But suddenly
they looked worried. "You're not going to
tell us to stop, are you?"

Percy glanced at the old rabbit.

"Well. . .no," he said to the mice.
"We just wondered if you could
have a marvellous time a little
more quietly?"

The mice cheered.

"We'll try!" they squeaked loudly.

"Come on," said Percy to the rabbit. "I think I've got some cotton wool in my bag. A little in each ear should do the trick."

THE FOX'S HICCUPS

The first stars were beginning to show in the sky as Percy the park keeper made his way home to his hut in the park.

He had been working hard all day and he was tired and hungry. Now he was looking forward to his supper and a good rest.

As Percy plodded on he saw his friend the fox coming up the path towards him. The fox was on his way home too.

"Good night," said Percy as they passed each other.

"Good night, hic-Percy," answered the fox.

The fox had hiccups.

The fox had been drinking some fizzy lemonade when a squirrel told him a funny joke about a parrot, a worm, and a cricket bat.

The fox exploded with laughter. It was then that he had learnt that it is not a good idea to laugh and drink at the same time. He had had hiccups all afternoon.

"I wonder if hic-Percy knows a good cure for hic-cups," the fox said to himself. "I th-hic I'll ask him," he said and with that he turned and followed after Percy.

W hen he got back to his hut, Percy
remembered that he still had one
or two jobs to do. First, he watered some
plants.

"I'd better get my washing in too,"
said Percy. "Then, it's two boiled eggs
for me and a pile of toast soldiers."

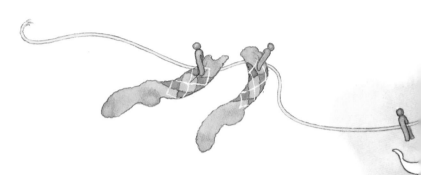

The fox hurried on. He wasn't afraid of the dark. He just liked the light better, that's all. But where was Percy?

He ran round the side of the hut, but instead of finding Percy, he found Percy's washing. Then, with a crash and a tumble which hurt his foot, he found a pile of flower pots.

"Oooowww-hic-ooww!" wailed the fox.

Percy was surprised by the crash. He stuck his head round the corner. But when Percy saw what had made the crash, he quickly pulled it back again.

"It's. . .it's a ghost!" he gasped.

Percy had never met a ghost before. He felt he should introduce himself. But what should he say to a ghost?

Percy listened hard. He could hear the ghost still moaning and thumping about. Suddenly, there was another loud crash, then silence.

Percy was just beginning to wonder if perhaps the ghost had disappeared when there came another sound. A small sound. It was not the sort of sound that Percy expected to hear from a ghost.

"Hic. . .burp."

A smile spread over Percy's face.

Percy poked his head round the corner again. This time, what he saw made him roar with laughter.

"Do you need any help, Mr Ghost?" said Percy, still laughing.

"Yes, please," came a muffled reply from inside the barrel. "Could you possibly turn me the right way up?"

Percy helped the fox back on to his feet. "You gave me quite a shock," said Percy.

"I gave myself one," said the fox. "But it seems to have cured my hiccups!"

THE BADGER'S BATH

The badger had been doing what badgers do best. Digging. He'd had a lovely day and, as usual when he'd had a lovely day, he was filthy dirty.

"I'm very sorry," said Percy the park keeper, "but you can't come to tea like that."

The badger looked disappointed.

"You'll just have to have a bath," said Percy.

The badger looked even more disappointed.

First, Percy filled a tin bath with warm soapy water. Then he brought out all the things that he liked to use himself when he had a bath. Soap, a loofah, his backbrush, a sponge, some shampoo and, of course, his rubber duck.

The badger sniffed at the soapy water. He didn't like it. He didn't like it at all.

Percy thought for a moment. Then he disappeared and came back with a jug which he used for wetting his hair and a shower cap which he used for not wetting it.

"There. I think that's everything," said
Percy. He turned to the badger.
"Now, all we need. . ." But the badger was
nowhere to be seen.

"Hmm. . ." said Percy. "Now all we need
is the badger."

The badger was hiding. He didn't want a bath.

Percy searched and searched but he couldn't find the badger anywhere. He was getting very hot and bothered.

"I really can't understand it," he said. "I always enjoy a bath myself."

$\mathbf{P}$ercy sighed as he looked at the bath full of soapy water. Then he had an idea. He went into his hut.

When Percy came out again he was wearing his swimming trunks.

"Well, why not?" he said to himself. He chuckled as he stepped out of his boots and into the bath.

Percy lay back in the warm water and gazed up through the overhanging branches of a tree.

"Silly old badger," thought Percy. "I wonder where he's hiding."

There was a sudden rustling above his head and something black and white moved amongst the leaves. A strange idea came into Percy's mind.

"No. . . surely not?" he said to himself. "Badgers don't climb trees. It must have been a magpie."

The rustling noise came again.

Suddenly, there was a loud CRACK!
With a great howl, a large black and
white animal fell out of the tree, straight
into Percy's bath water. SP-LOOSH!

For a moment, the badger completely disappeared. Then his head popped up through the soap suds, coughing and spluttering.

P ercy was spluttering too, but with
laughter.

"I see you changed your mind about
having a bath," he chuckled. "I suppose
you didn't want to miss your tea!"

"I didn't know badgers climbed trees," said Percy.

"Well," said the badger, "we're better at digging." He sighed. "Could you pass me the loofah, please?"

THE HEDGEHOG'S BALLOON

P ercy the park keeper looked up from
his work and gazed in wonder.
"Two red ones. . . a blue one. . . there's
a yellow one. . . and another blue one. . ."

Percy was counting balloons. "I wonder where they're coming from," he said to himself. "Somebody must have had a party."

He put down his trowel and wiped his hands.

"Well, if nobody wants them," he said, "I think I'll help myself."

Percy chased after the balloons as they floated past him on the breeze. It didn't take him long to collect as many as he could carry.

He began to walk back towards his hut, whistling happily.

Suddenly, Percy stopped. He could hear a faint sound coming from a tree stump nearby. It was not a happy sound.

"Someone's crying," said Percy. "Oh dear." He let go of his balloons and hurried over to the stump.

Sitting on the tree stump, and looking very upset, was a hedgehog. Two mice were doing their best to comfort him.

"Goodness me," said Percy. "Whatever is the matter?"

"It's all these balloons," said the hedgehog.

Then, in between sniffs and sobs, he explained to Percy how he had always loved balloons. The trouble was that he could never have them because they would always burst on his spines.

"It's just not fair!" And the hedgehog burst into tears again.

"You poor thing," said Percy. He tried to put his arm around the hedgehog but took it away at once.

"Ouch," he said.

Then Percy took one of his thick gardening gloves out of his pocket and put it on. The hedgehog nestled into his hand.

"I think everyone should be able to play with balloons," said Percy. "And that includes hedgehogs."

He put on the other glove and gently carried the hedgehog towards an old store shed. The two mice followed.

The mice watched Percy through the window. He set the hedgehog down on a workbench and then he took a tin from a shelf. He opened the lid.

"What's Percy doing?" said one of the mice. "What's in that box?"

"I don't know," said the other mouse. "I can't see properly."

The mice didn't have to wait long to find out. Percy picked up the hedgehog and brought him outside.

"There!" said Percy. "A good idea, even if I say so myself! I think those balloons will be safe now."

The mice clapped and the hedgehog beamed. He thought how smart he must look, wearing his corks.

P ercy caught hold of a bright yellow
   balloon.
   "Here you are," said Percy as he
handed it to the hedgehog. "Your very
first balloon."

The hedgehog took the balloon and
with a great big smile on his face,
he scampered off with the balloon floating
beside him.

"Another satisfied customer," said
Percy, feeling pleased with himself.

Percy turned to go back to his hut. But suddenly, there came a loud BANG!

"Oops!" said Percy. "One of the corks must have come off. It's a good job we've got plenty of balloons!"

"Don't worry," Percy called to the hedgehog, "I'm coming. . ."